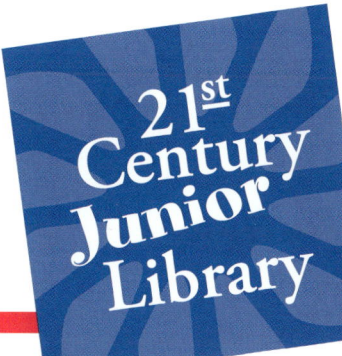

Visit the Doctor!

by Katie Marsico

CHERRY LAKE PUBLISHING * ANN ARBOR, MICHIGAN

Published in the United States of America by Cherry Lake Publishing
Ann Arbor, Michigan
www.cherrylakepublishing.com

Content Adviser: Charisse Gencyuz, M.D., Clinical Instructor, Department of Internal Medicine, University of Michigan.

Reading Adviser: Marla Conn, ReadAbility, Inc

Photo Credits: © castillodominici/Thinkstock Photos, cover; © Blend Images/Shutterstock Images, 4; © Image Point Fr/Shutterstock Images, 6; © michaeljung/Shutterstock Images, 8; © Pavel L Photo and Video/Shutterstock Images, 10; © Rob Byron/Shutterstock Images, 12; © Syda Productions/Shutterstock Images, 14; © Condor 36/Shutterstock Images, 16; © bikeriderlondon/Shutterstock Images, 18; © Becky Wass/Shutterstock Photos, 20

Copyright ©2015 by Cherry Lake Publishing
All rights reserved. No part of this book may be reproduced or utilized in any form or by any means without written permission from the publisher.

LIBRARY OF CONGRESS CATALOGING-IN-PUBLICATION DATA

Marsico, Katie, 1980-
 Visit the doctor! / by Katie Marsico.
      pages cm. – (Your healthy body)
 Includes index.
 Audience: 6-10
 Audience: K to grade 3
 ISBN 978-1-63188-985-1 (hardcover)—ISBN 978-1-63362-063-6 (pdf)—ISBN 978-1-63362-024-7 (pbk.)—ISBN 978-1-63362-102-2 (ebook)
 1. Children–Medical examinations–Juvenile literature.
 2. Children–Preparation for medical care–Juvenile literature. I. Title.
 RJ50.5.M35 2015
 618.92'0075–dc23   2014021523

Cherry Lake Publishing would like to acknowledge the work of
The Partnership for 21st Century Skills.
Please visit www.p21.org for more information.

Printed in the United States of America
Corporate Graphics

CONTENTS

5 **Wondering in the Waiting Room**

11 **A Better Look at the Body**

17 **What the Doctor Does**

22 Glossary

23 Find Out More

24 Index

24 About the Author

Checkups are a chance to learn more about your body and the best ways to stay healthy.

Wondering in the Waiting Room

Avi sits in Dr. Tam's waiting room and sighs. Dr. Tam is a pediatrician, or a doctor who treats children. Avi likes her. But he doesn't understand why he's

Think about the last time you visited a doctor. Were you sick or well? What did the doctor do during your exam? What did he or she say about your health?

Your doctor will probably ask if you have any health problems that you want to talk about.

visiting her today. After all, he's not sick. He hopes he doesn't need any shots either. Avi's mom reminds him that people don't see doctors just when they're ill. Regular checkups are an important part of building a healthy body.

Doctors are trained to practice medicine. Sometimes this involves **diagnosing** and

Look! Look at this photo of a pediatrician with a patient. What is the doctor doing? Why is this an important part of a regular checkup?

Some doctors only take care of babies.

treating diseases and injuries. Doctors also work with patients to prevent illness. They give people advice about caring for their bodies.

Checkups allow pediatricians to see how their patients are growing. Kids and parents can discuss any health concerns they have, too. Kids over three years old usually need only one checkup a year.

Other patients have health conditions that doctors want to check often. Most doctors tell people to call or visit any time they have health questions.

During a checkup, a nurse will measure how much you've grown since your last appointment.

10

A Better Look at the Body

Nurse Hamby says it's time for Avi's exam. First, she asks him to step onto a scale in the hallway. She records his weight in a chart. Next, she measures his height.

Then they go into the exam room. Nurse Hamby tells Avi to climb onto the examination table. She places a Velcro cuff on his arm. A machine attached to the

These medical tools are all often used during checkups. Are you able to guess what each one does?

cuff measures his **blood pressure**. This helps the nurse see how well his heart is pumping blood. The cuff squeezes Avi's arm. It doesn't hurt, though.

Next, it's time to check Avi's temperature. Nurse Hamby places a thermometer under his tongue. It beeps, and she removes it. Avi's temperature is 98.7 degrees Fahrenheit (37.1 degrees Celsius). That is just what it should be.

If you have a fever, your temperature will be higher than normal.

Nurse Hamby is done with her part of the exam! She walks out of the room with Avi's chart. She puts it in a holder by the door. She says Dr. Tam will review her notes and will be in shortly!

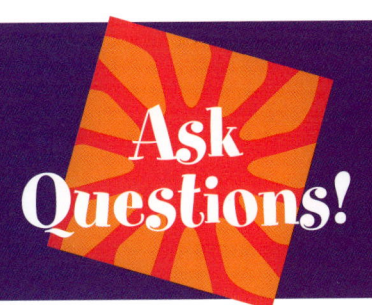

Ask a nurse what a healthy body temperature should be. A very high or very low temperature can be a sign of being sick. Temperatures are often taken with an **oral** thermometer.

Your doctor will listen to your heart and lungs with a stethoscope.

What the Doctor Does

Avi hears a knock at the door. It's Dr. Tam! She says hello and opens up Avi's chart. Dr. Tam tells Avi he is growing well. His blood pressure is normal for someone his age. Dr. Tam places her **stethoscope**

Have you ever gotten a shot during a checkup? If so, can you guess why? Did you say it was because you were getting a vaccination? You'd probably be right! Vaccinations contain substances that help protect people from different diseases.

When testing your reflexes, your doctor will watch how your legs move.

on Avi's chest. She asks him to breathe deeply. She's listening to his heart and lungs. Dr. Tam uses an **otoscope** to get a closer look at Avi's ears, nose, and throat. She studies his eyes with an **ophthalmoscope**. She taps his knees with a small rubber hammer. This tests Avi's **reflexes**.

Finally, she gently pushes on Avi's stomach and back with her hands. She makes sure none of his inner **organs** are swollen, and that his spine isn't curved.

Visiting the doctor regularly will help you stay healthy!

Good news! Avi is a healthy boy! Dr. Tam asks what questions he and his mom have. Avi asks if he needs any vaccinations today. Luckily, Dr. Tam says no. Avi won't need shots until his next checkup. He thanks her. He's glad she's helping him build a healthy body!

Create!

Create a timeline of your health and growth. Ask your parents if they have records from your old checkups. Record the dates of your checkups on poster board. List important information you have from each exam.

GLOSSARY

blood pressure (BLUHD PREH-shuhr) the force with which blood flows through a person's body

diagnosing (DYE-ig-nohs-ing) using an exam to recognize a disease or illness

ophthalmoscope (ahf-THAL-muh-skope) an instrument that features a mirror and light that are used to examine the inner eye

oral (OR-uhl) done or taken by way of the mouth

organs (OR-guhnz) body parts such as the intestines that perform a specific job

otoscope (OH-tuh-skope) an instrument that features a light and a set of lenses that are used to examine the ears, nose, and throat

reflexes (REE-fleks-uhz) body motions that happen automatically as a reaction to something

stethoscope (STEH-thuh-skope) an instrument that allows people to more closely listen to sounds made by the heart and lungs

FIND OUT MORE

BOOKS

Dawson, Patricia A. *A Doctor's Job*. New York: Cavendish Square Publishing, 2015.

Kuskowski, Alex. *Cool Body Basics: Healthy and Fun Ways to Care for Your Body*. Minneapolis: ABDO Publishing Company, 2013.

Minden, Cecilia. *Nurses*. Mankato, MN: The Child's World, 2014.

WEB SITES

BC (British Columbia) Children's Hospital—How the Body Works
www.aboutkidshealth.ca/BCCH/En/HowTheBodyWorks/Pages/default.aspx
Explore animated maps of your body that are sure to come in handy the next time you visit the doctor!

KidsHealth—Going to the Doctor
kidshealth.org/kid/feel_better/people/going_to_dr.html
Learn more details about what occurs during a checkup, and get links to other online articles about kids' health.

INDEX

A
blood pressure, 13, 17

C
checkups, 4, 7, 9

D
diagnosing, 7

F
fever, 14

H
heart, 13, 16, 19
height, 10, 11

I
illness prevention, 9

L
lungs, 16, 19

N
nurse, 10, 11–15

O
ophthalmoscope, 19
organs, inner, 19
otoscope, 19

P
pediatrician, 5, 9

R
reflexes, 18, 19

S
shots, 17, 21
stethoscope, 16, 17

T
temperature, 13, 14

V
vaccinations, 17, 21

W
weight, 11

ABOUT THE AUTHOR

Katie Marsico is the author of more than 150 children's books. She lives in a suburb of Chicago, Illinois, with her husband and children.

24

J 610 MAR

Marsico, Katie, 1980-

Visit the doctor!

APR 0 2 2015